The Christmas Star

Chandra Felisa Wallace

All other highlighted words are defined in the back of this book.

Enjoy!!!

ISBN 978-1-64258-281-9 (paperback)
ISBN 978-1-64258-282-6 (digital)

Christian Faith Publishing, Inc.
832 Park Avenue
Meadville, PA 16335
www.christianfaithpublishing.com

Printed in the United States of America

The heavens declare the glory of God, and the firmament shows His handiwork. Day unto day utters His speech, and the night reveals His knowledge. The midnight galaxy was all lit up with shining stars beaming down on earth because He was coming! Their presence was magnificent and glorious. The planets and moon were in their rightful place, so beautiful to behold. How excellent is His works in all His creation! All was merry and joyous with great expectation and excitement, until… wait. What was that? He heard a very pitiful, sorrowful, and painful cry. Well, He in His infinite wisdom, and He being omniscient realized immediately it was coming from none other than His precious, adorable Little Star.

Her eyes were closed as she said through sorrowful tears, "Star light. Star bright.

I wish I could be that beautiful star that shines so bright!" Then she slowly opened her eyes and gave herself a glance over and said sternly, still crying though, "I'm not because I'm little, and no one notices me! *Ugh!*" She said, "I feel bad because I want to be a star that's significant! I want to be a star that's relevant! I want to be special! Popular! A big deal, with lots of attention poured on me, like everyone else because I WANT TO MATTER!!!"

She sighed, took a deep breath to try and calm herself down but continued to vent. "If only I had a plan and purpose for my life, like everybody else in the universe! If only I was born to be someone who shined everywhere they went like Santa Claus. If only I was created to do something special with my life, like Rudolph the red nose reindeer, or the little drummer boy, or even that show-off planet Pluto!

"But no surprise here, it isn't happening, and I don't understand why! Did I do something bad in my past I'm not aware of, like not say *thank you* or *please*? Or was it because I insisted that the Starfish change his name to Randolph! Or was it when I offered Santa's elves a mint and some chap stick. What could possibly be the reason you made me this way, Lord? Why did you make me a no nothing of a star that is basically…invisible?" Little Star continued on her sad melancholy rant, "Why, Lord? Help me to understand? Why you won't let this little light of mine to shine, shine, shine?"

Melancholy: [mel-*uh* n-kol-ee]
A gloomy state of mind, especially when habitual or prolonged; depression.

And the Lord responded with loving kindness and tender mercies. "Oh my precious Little Star, don't you know everything I created is good and perfect? Everything I created is significant and definitely relevant. And most importantly, everything I created ALL matters to Me, which makes it ALL a very big deal. That is why I'm doing what I'm doing, my darling Little Star. The entire world will know what "appears" to be powerless, insignificant, **impoverished,** or even common, without any pomp and circumstance, is the GREATEST GIFT that I'm giving to the world and mankind. A baby!"

The Word of the LORD in Luke 2:1–5 reads:

> *And it came to pass in those days that a **decree** went out from Caesar Augustus that all the world should be registered. This **census** first took place while Quirinius was governing Syria. So all went to be registered, everyone to his own city, Joseph also went up from Galilee, out of the city of Nazareth, into Judea, to the city of David, which is called Bethlehem, because he was of the house and **lineage** of David, to be registered with Mary, his **betrothed** wife, who was with child.*

Betrothed: [bih-troh*th* d,-trawtht] Engaged to be married
Lineage: ˈlinēij ancestry · family · parentage · birth · descent · line pedigree

Joseph told Mary to please hang in there. He said to his beloved, "Mary, I know we've been searching for a good while now, but I won't stop until I find us a place to stay. I'm praying there are still a few places left for us to lodge that are close by. Let's go across town and see if they have a room for us there. Don't worry Mary, my love, I'm going to take real good care of you."

Mary wanted to assure Joseph that she had complete trust in him. She knew she was chosen for greatness, and Joseph was a part of that plan. She told him, "Joseph, my dear. I'm not worried at all. I know you'll take good care of me." Something inside her told her everything would work together for their good, and she found great comfort in knowing they were called for something special! Called for such a time as this!

So they continued on their journey, a little wearied but undaunted about the task ahead. They came to what appeared to be an impoverished town. They saw a dim candlelight on in the window of one of the inns. Joseph got excited and quickly knocked on the door. The innkeeper opened the door and greeted them both.

Joseph, being a just man, used his best pleasantry. "Good evening, kind sir. May we please rent a room from you tonight?"

The innkeeper quickly sized up the young couple and saw that the young woman was very pregnant. He hated to give them the news that he didn't have a vacancy, so he reluctantly said to Joseph, "I'm sorry Sir, but we're all filled up here. There are no more vacancies. Since Caesar Augustus ordered the decree for the census, we've been booked up solid for weeks. You might have a chance with the lady down the street. Again, my apologies. I bid you a good night and good luck." He glanced again at Mary and said, "You're sure going to need it!"

Joseph sighed with deep frustration. He knew Mary was tired and needed to rest. But something inside him told him to keep looking and not to grow weary in well doing. He had a dream where an angel appeared to him and told him so. So he stayed positive because he knew inside his heart it was going to be all right.

Undaunted: [ənˈdôn(t)əd]
not intimidated or discouraged by difficulty, danger, or disappointment.

Joseph set out again on the journey with Mary by his side. This time he was more determined than ever to **persevere** and find them a place to stay. He knew he could not fail. He was inspired by the dream he had with the angel who told him to take care of Mary because the Child she was carrying was special. He saw another candle burning in the window of an inn up ahead. They quickly went there and walked right up to the front door and knocked. A lady with a beautiful smile answered the door.

Joseph said to the nice lady, "How are you doing, ma'am. My beloved and I really, really need a place to stay tonight. We searched everywhere and can't find any vacancies. Can you please, please help us out?" Joseph knew he sounded desperate, but at this point, he didn't care. He would beg and plead if he had to, to get his precious Mary in her delicate state off those cold, damp streets!

The kind innkeeper looked at them **woefully** and said, "Oh, I wish I could Sir, but everything is booked up in this little town of Bethlehem." Joseph felt despair creep all over him and began to lose all hope. Then the innkeeper said,

"Wow, your beloved is with child! I can't in good conscience, let you two wander the streets with her in that condition." The innkeeper thought long and hard. "Wait, I may have a solution to your problem, but it's not a very good one, I suppose. The only thing I have left to offer you is my barn where I keep some of my animals. I know it's not the best accommodations for you and your beloved, Sir, but at least it will get you out of the cold, and you'll have a roof over your heads for the time being. You're more than welcome to stay there if you like. I'm sorry. I wish I could offer you better."

Joseph looked at Mary. He lowered his head and said, "Mary, my love, I'm afraid this is our only option. I've looked everywhere! All the inns are booked up solid. I'm so sorry I couldn't find us a better place to stay. But you need to rest and get out of the cold! I feel as though I've failed you." Mary told Joseph never in a million years would she ever think he's failed her. She knew God had provided for them! Something inside her told her that. She said to her wonderful betrothed Joseph, "We'll be just fine right here, Joseph. Right here in this little town of Bethlehem."

Persevere: /ˌpərsəˈvir/
Continue in a course of action even in the face of difficulty: not giving up!

Little Star cleared her throat quickly and said, "Wow, Lord! Why couldn't I have been born to be Joseph! I would have found a better place to stay than him! My goodness! A barn with field animals! And you made him shine? Even if you made me, Mary, I would have been so happy to tell Joseph it was an epic fail! The barn just would not do! I would have insisted on better accommodations and shined in the process. Lord, I just want to be somebody special like them and do something great with my life. I would have even settled to be the innkeeper who had the barn. My goodness, even she had purpose. She had the barn! I just want to be significant like them, Lord. I just want to shine!"

So the Lord, who is **omnipotent,** gave Little Star the imagination of what it would be like to be Joseph with all his responsibilities of providing for Mary and his **impending** family. Little Star quickly realized that being Joseph was harder than she imagined. Joseph worked hard for the things he needed to provide for his family. Little Star didn't mind a little work here or there, but a lot of work everywhere did not quite fit into her immediate plans! So Little Star pleaded her case to the Lord that it would be far better if she were Mary.

The Lord is gracious, **merciful,** and slow to anger. He again opened Little Star's imagination, and she learned very quickly that Mary was **humble, demure,** and very soft-spoken. Totally in sharp contrast of what Little Star loved to be. She loved to speak her mind! She loved to have an opinion! Demure was not even in her vocabulary. So it was obvious she made a mistake in wanting to be Mary. It was clear, however, that she should be the innkeeper with the barn.

Right away, her imagination kicked in, and she was the keeper of the inn. People were coming by all day long and asking her questions, and complaining about why this was that way and why that wasn't this way! Her head began to ache and spin. She realized that Joseph, Mary, and the innkeeper were called to be who they are. But she felt in no uncertain terms that she was NOT to be who she is! And sadness settled all over her again.

Demure: /dəˈmyŏŏr/
modest, unassuming, meek, mild, reserved, retiring, quiet, shy, bashful

The Word of the Lord in Luke 2:6–7 reads:

*"So it was that while they were there, the days were completed for her to be delivered. And she brought forth her firstborn Son, and wrapped Him in **swaddling** cloths, and laid Him in a manger, because there was no room for them in the inn."*

The Lord said, "Everyone and everything has a purpose, my darling Little Star. It's all by My design. There was no crib for His bed, like He didn't even matter, but that was all by My design. My sweet precious Little Star, stay joyful and triumphant! A Child is born this day in the city of Bethlehem! Oh My precious, lovely Little Star, please understand that My ways are not your ways, nor are my thoughts, your thoughts, so lean not to your own understanding. Know this my precious Little Star. it's all by My design!"

Mary and Joseph praised God for their bundle of great joy. A beautiful baby boy so tender and mild. They both knew that this Child was special. This Child was extraordinary! Mary gathered the child in her arms, and unbeknownst to her, a young child angel sang a beautiful, lovely lullaby of praise to the Newborn King. Mary rocked her baby to sleep in heavenly peace. What a silent night. What a Holy night.

The child angel sang, *"What Child is this who laid to rest, On Mary's lap is sleeping? Whom angels greet with anthem sweet, While shepherds watch are keeping? This, this is Christ the King whom shepherds guard and angels sing. Haste, haste to bring Him laud, The Babe, the Son of Mary."*

Unbeknownst: /ənbəˈnōn st/
Happening or existing without the knowledge of; unaware of something

"Wow!" Little Star said. "Why couldn't I have been given the gift to sing like that kid? If I were a singing star, then I would really shine! Just go ahead and give me my **Grammy**! Or better yet, if I were a baby, like that beautiful, glorious baby, I would really, really, shine, shine, shine! Lord, do You even love me? Because if you did, then you would have made me to be more like them instead of more like me. Being me is not fun at all!" she whined!

The Lord heard Little Star loud and clear. So He caused a deep sleep to come over her. She dreamed deeply of being a fabulous singer. In her dream, she sang and she sang and she sang until, wait a minute…she didn't want to sing anymore! And what was all this funny business about rehearsing and hitting higher notes! Any second now, she felt her vocal cords come tumbling out of her mouth! The dream of being a fabulous singer became a less-than-fabulous nightmare! She realized that singing was not at all she had dreamt it to be. But God is good because now in her dream, she was a little bitty, cuddly baby that everyone seemed to love and cherish.

Grammy: /ˈgramē/
A Grammy Award is an honor awarded by The Recording Academy to recognize outstanding achievement in the music industry.

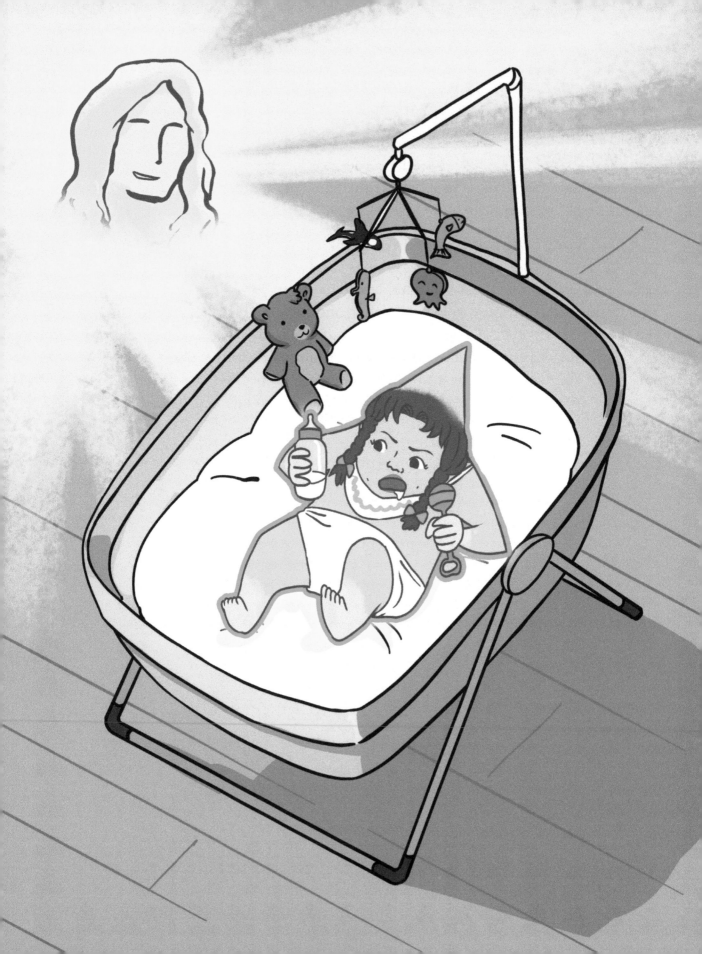

Finally, she had all the attention she's always wanted! But there was this one little thing getting in the way of her contentment. Why, oh why, did she have to drink milk all day and all the time! Couldn't she just eat a nice juicy steak? Or how about some nachos with cheese? She figured it out. How about strawberry cheesecake. It's soft, right? Milk? With no chocolate flavoring! And for some strange reason, she constantly dribbled all over her neck and clothes. YUCK! Also, she felt compelled to scream at the top of her lungs. That was sort of fun but **undignified** if you know what I mean. "Um, Lord," said Little Star. "I changed my mind about being a baby. Babies are kind of, I don't know ….WEIRD! Can I please wake up now to my sad, depressed way of living to my sad, depressed way of life?"

Undignified: /ənˈdɪgnəˌfɪd/
demeaning, unbecoming, unworthy, degrading, shameful, dishonorable, unsuitable

The Lord told His darling Little Star that He loves her more than she'll ever know. He said, "I'll allow my Son to do the ultimate sacrifice for you and mankind because of my love for you, Little Star. He will lay down His life for you. My Son is the Light of the world. This Gift I'm giving is my greatest Gift ever! He is the most special Gift of all time to all mankind. For unto you a Child is born. Unto you a Son is given, and the government will be on His shoulders. And His name shall be called Wonderful, Counselor, Prince of Peace, Mighty God, and Everlasting Father! Little Star, I want you to know I made no mistake when I created you. Oh come now, let us worship and adore HIM! BORN THE KING OF ANGELS, BORN THE KING OF KINGS!!!"

They both looked down upon the **nativity** scene at the baby lying in the manger. Above them high in the sky was His mark that told the world the Savior was born!

Nativity: /nəˈtivədē/
The occasion of a person's birth. A picture, carving, or model representing Jesus Christ's birth.

The Word of the LORD in Luke 2:8 reads:

> *"Now there were in the same country shepherds living out in the fields, keeping watch over their flock by night."*

All the shepherds were lying down in the field looking up into the starry night, and the first shepherd said, "What a wonderful evening tonight. The stars are brightly shining. It feels like something special is in the air!"

They all agreed, and the second shepherd said, "It's like heaven and nature singing because God and sinners **reconciled**. Wow! Look at that great big star! It's really bright and shining!"

"WHAT!!!" shouted Little Star.

Another shepherd said, "It looks like it's over Bethlehem!"

The first shepherd said very nervously, "OMG, you guys. What in the world is that? Shepherds quake at that sight!" All the shepherds **cowered** to their knees shaking, greatly afraid. One covered his eyes, another covered his head, and the last one screamed, "Don't hurt us!"

The Word of the LORD in Luke 2:9–10 reads:

> *"And behold, an angel of the Lord stood before them, and the glory of the Lord shone around them, and they were greatly afraid. The angel said to them ...."*

"Do not be afraid, for behold, I bring you good tidings of great joy which will be to all people. For there is born to you this day in the city of David a Savior, who is Christ the Lord. And this will be the sign to you: You will find a Babe wrapped in swaddling clothes, lying in a manger."

The Word of the Lord in Luke 2:13–14 reads:

> *"And suddenly there was with the angel a multitude of the heavenly host praising God and saying...Glory to God in the highest, And on earth peace, goodwill toward men!"*

Cower: ˈ/kou(ə)r/
tremble, shake, quake, shrink, recoil, shy away

Everywhere the shepherds looked were angels. There were big angels and little angels called cherubim of all sizes, shapes, and skin colors. They were all very beautiful and glorious. As the heavenly host of angels praised the Most High God, the whole creation was in a state of majesty, where the creation spoke highly of its Creator! The Father and His Holy Spirit gave great praise to the newborn King! Joy to the world, the Lord has come! Let earth receive her King!

Then all was well with the shepherds because God did not give them a spirit of fear, but of power, love, and a sound mind. Something told them inside their hearts that they were about to witness something more glorious in splendor than the host of heavenly angels. Something told them inside their hearts that the world as they knew it would never be the same. There was such love in the air. This was a love they could not deny. This was a love they all wanted to partake of!

Cherubim: ˈ/CHerəb/
a winged angelic being described in biblical tradition as attending on God

Little Star lamented, "Oh, come on, Lord! You used a star, and you didn't use me? Okay, okay, I know why, because I'm little. Isn't it? That star is gigantic and really unusually bright! Unlike me! It's so unfair! I would have lit up heaven and earth all by myself if you made me like that star on steroids! You know, Lord, I would have made a great angel too. I know how to **proclaim**! I know how to scare shepherds! I would have shined as an angel of the Lord! I would have shined if I just wasn't me. Did you hear me, Lord? If-I-just-was-not-me!"

Then the Lord said to His petulant, yet **precocious**, adorable Little Star, "Oh I hear you, my darling, and your **sentiments** are very clear. My ears are attentive to those I love."

So the Almighty caused Little Star to see a vision that was crystal clear. She was that gigantic star that hovered above the galaxy and glowed magnificently above all the other stars. "Oh my goodness," she said. "I'm not little anymore!" And best of all, she was glowing, almost like …shining! But she was glowing all by herself way out there all alone. All the other stars were far below her star, and they weren't looking up at her like she wanted them to. She looked in the distance to her left and saw the moon shining bright. It was shining even more than she was glowing. *Um that's not good,* she thought.

The moon also was all by itself, although the moon seemed content to be all by itself. It seemed like the moon was proud to be doing what it was created to do. She didn't quite understand how the moon wasn't uncomfortable being alone way out there by itself. She didn't like being alone. She wanted company! Lots of company and someone to talk to on a regular basis because she was a professional runner of the mouth with always something to say! But, by golly, she was glowing, and she was *big!* So why did she feel "uncomfortable and tense." She thought where out here could she go to get a neck massage.

She started to feel another serious problem coming into view. She wanted to be amongst the other stars, so they and planet Pluto could see what a *big* deal she was, but she was too big and needed more room way out in the galaxy. She wanted to glow amongst her friends, but her glow was too glorious because of her size. What's a star to do?

Precocious: [pri-koh-shuh s]
Unusually advanced or mature in development, especially mental development

She thought about it long and hard and decided, maybe in about twenty years or more, she'll be a gigantic star that glows, but right now she thought it would be better if she were an angel! Then she learned that angels are sent out on assignment, and most of the assignments are not by choice. To be an angel required flexibility and an openness to be wherever became available. She thought she could choose to do her assignment in Paris, France, or San Trope', or the beaches of the **Caribbean**. But she learned her assignment could well be going to impoverished Haiti, or the Russian slums, or even the Artic North Pole! Well, that's great for Santa and the elves, but not so great for her. Just the very thought of it gave her goosebumps! Well, not to be an undecided, "under-achiever believer," she knew she aimed for happiness, and the angel thing did not seem so heavenly!

"My lovely and precious Little Star," said the Lord. "You are fearfully and wonderfully made. I knew you before you were. I have hedged you behind and before and laid My hand upon you. Such knowledge is too wonderful for you, Little Star. It is high, and you cannot attain it. Marvelous are My works and My soul knows very well. I will lead you in the way everlasting. My darling, precious Little Star."

The shepherds all realized they needed to follow the glorious star to Bethlehem. They all wanted to see the great thing which had come to pass. The shepherds knew the Lord Himself had made this known to them!

The Word of the LORD in Luke 2:16–18, 20 reads:
> *And they came with haste and found Mary and Joseph and the Babe lying in a manger. Now when they had seen Him, they made widely known the saying which was told them concerning this Child. And all those who heard it **marveled** at those things which were told them by the shepherds. Then the shepherds returned, glorifying and praising God for all the things that they had heard and seen, as it was told them.*

And one of the shepherds said, "C'mon you guys let's go and tell it on the mountains and everywhere that Jesus Christ is born!"

The **Caribbean** is a region that consists of the Caribbean Sea, its islands, and the surrounding coasts. The region is southeast of the Gulf of Mexico and the North American mainland, east of Central America, and north of South America. It's a desired vacation because of the warm water.

Little Star was amazed by how significant the shepherds were! She said to the Lord, "You know, Lord, if I was born a shepherd, I would be out in the fields and mountains breathing fresh air and telling the sheep what to do. I would be a BOSS! But not just any ole BOSS, I would be a shepherd BOSS that shines!" Then she realized her **predicament** and said, "Who am I kidding? I'll never do anything special like those shepherds. They have character, and I don't. If I could do something great like them, everyone would know how important I am, including the sheep! I would be significant as a shepherd! I just want you to understand, Lord, I want to matter! And, of course, shine in the process too."

The Lord looked at His precious Little Star and said, "Seriously my darling Little Star, do you really want to be a shepherd? Do you know all the things shepherds have to do?"

"Yeah, they **shear** the sheep, right?" Little Star replied.

"Yes, ALL the sheep," said the Lord.

"You mean the whole gazillion herd?" asked Little Star.

"Yes," the Lord said. "And do you know what else they have to do?"

"They have to clean up all their…" Little Star went silent.

The Lord lovingly said, "Yes, my precious. Shepherds have to clean it ALL up."

Little Star turned purple! She felt **queasy**. When she realized all the responsibilities of the shepherds, without question Little Star knew shearing, and especially shoveling, was not her thing! "Uh, Lord? I need to sit down and take a moment to reevaluate and, most importantly, recover from the shepherd thing."

Predicament: [prəˈdikəmənt]
a difficult, unpleasant, or embarrassing situation.

The Lord said, "My adorable Little Star. To everything there is a season; a time for every purpose under heaven; a time to speak, and a time to be silent."

"Oh. I'm sorry, Lord," said Little Star as she motioned to zip her lips.

"No, precious, I wasn't finished," explained the Lord. "There comes a time to weep and there comes a time to laugh. A time to lose and a time to gain. A time to mourn and a time to dance! Always, always a time to LOVE, and finally, a time to be born! This, this is CHRIST THE KING, whom shepherds guard and angels sing!"

The Word of the LORD reads in Matthew 2:1–3, 7

> *Now after Jesus was born in Bethlehem of Judea, in the days of Herod the king, behold, wise men from the East came to Jerusalem saying… Where is He who has been born King of the Jews? For we have seen His star in the East and have come to worship Him. When Herod the king heard this, he was troubled, and all Jerusalem with him. Then Herod, when he had secretly called the wise men, determined from them what time the star appeared.*

"Knock, knock, knock. It's us, Mr. King Herod, your local friendly, and "wise" *(they used finger quotes every time they said the word "wise")* astronomers!" said the first wise man.

"Come on in, gentlemen, and have a seat," said King Herod. "I heard you all were passing through and following that star everyone is talking about. Is that true, and when exactly did that star appear?"

"Well, you know, KH," said the second wise man. "Is it all right if I call you that?"

"No," said King Herod.

"Well, I knew it was 'wise' to ask. As I was saying, Mr. King Herod, it would be foolish of us to try to determine the exact time of the star's appearance even though we are astronomers. But we can determine 'wisely' it's over Bethlehem of Judea."

Astronomers: as·tron·o·mer
Astronomers are **scientists** who study the Universe and everything about stars, planets, and galaxies.

King Herod retorted, "I heard you three have all the answers. I also heard a special Child was born and is worshipped by many, and that star has something to do with it. Some crazy, foolish people are even calling Him the King of kings, when everybody knows that's me! But I ain't mad at nobody. I just want to pay my respects to the Child *(he smiled wickedly)*. That's all. So I thought when you three find the Child, you'll come right back here and let me know EXACTLY where he is so I could go and worship Him too, you know, King to…**King-Pin**!"

The third wise man said, "Well, Mr. King Herod, we think that's just *awful-ly* kind of you. It's probably 'wise' of us to be on our way. Wisdom teaches that haste is not waste. A journey of a thousand miles begins with one step. Hickory, dickory dock the—"

"I get it!" Snarled King Herod.

"Okay then, Mr. King Herod, we're off toward the journey. It will be 'wise' of us to travel the roads of wisdom. Good day, sir."

And the Word of the LORD reads in Matthew 1:9–11:

When they heard the king, they departed: and behold, the star which they had seen in the East went before them, till it came and stood over where the young Child was. When they saw the star, they rejoiced with exceedingly great joy. And when they had come into the house, they saw the young Child with Mary His mother, and fell down and worshiped Him.

King-Pin
A dastardly fictional supervillain or a gangster, mob boss, or crime lord.

"Hallelujah, my friends and fellow astronomers!" said the first wise man. "It was 'wise' of us to follow the star. The Holy Spirit, who is the wisest of the wise, told us the Savior was born, and here He is! Praise His holy name! I thought it 'wise' of me to bring Him my gift of gold!" He placed his gift of gold next to the baby Jesus.

The second wise man exclaimed joyfully, "Glory to God, my humble friends and fellow astronomers! Not only was that a great idea but a 'wise' idea indeed. What a beautiful Child! He is a joy to the world! I also thought it equally 'wise' to bring Him my gift of frankincense." He handed his gift to Joseph.

The third wise man chimed in and said, "Yes, my fellow colleagues and esteemed astronomers, the Child is worthy of all honor, praise, and glory! I must say, I find both of you to be very 'wise' in your choice of gifts. It was 'wise' of us to travel so far to see this great and awesome sight! Being that I'm considered to be extremely 'wise' in my decision-making, I brought Him my gift of myrrh." Then the third wise man handed his gift of myrrh to Mary, the mother of Jesus.

"A 'wise' choice indeed!" said the first wise man merrily. "Now, gentleman, we must be on our way. I was divinely warned in a dream. King Herod is waiting for us to report back to him about the Child. He has very bad intentions. I think it 'wise' of us to NOT tell him anything! Let's go home another way. A road far less traveled."

The second wise man agreed with his comrade and said, "My dear sir and fellow astronomer, again you have spoken 'wisely.'"

"Amen and amen again!" declared the third wise man.

Colleagues: col·league
A fellow member of a profession, staff, or academic faculty; an associate

Joy to the world!

"You know, Lord," said Little Star. "I want to be many things, but I know I do not want to be King Herod! But a wise astronomer will work just fine for me! What I could do with all that wisdom, not to mention all the attention I would get with it! Everyone would say, 'I see you, Little Star, who is wise with all the answers! I would tell KH he should…'"

"Excuse me, Little Star," interrupted the Lord. "It would be 'wise' for you to listen right now."

The angel appeared in the heavens and declared His name was called JESUS, the name given by the angel before He was conceived in the womb.

Little Star looked confused. "Lord, I don't get it. If this is Christ the King, you should have made him shine more. He should have been born in royalty, splendor, and wealth. That way, he really would be shining!"

The Lord smiled at His precious Little Star. "My sweet, absolutely adorable Little Star, Jesus may not have been born in royalty, **splendor,** and wealth, but because He is my Child, He already has royalty, splendor, and wealth in Him. Perception is not always reality. Little Star, you have to understand even though at the moment you don't have something you want or need, that something you're lacking can be attained through your own potential and perseverance. It's already in you! My Son will shine brightly in the hearts of all who believe in Him."

Splendor: /splendə/
magnificence, luxury, richness, fineness, lavishness, glory, beauty, elegance

Little Star looked down on the baby Jesus again and noticed someone new had come on the scene. Little Star pointed at that person and said, "Lord, who is that old man?"

The Lord happily said, "One of My shining saints! Oh, the joy that floods My soul!"

Little Star wasn't unhappy because someone else was shining; she was curious. What was it about this man for the Lord to refer to him as one of His shining saints?

And the Word of the Lord in Luke 2:25–28 reads:

> *And behold, there was a man in Jerusalem whose name was Simeon, and this man was just and devout, waiting for the **Consolation** of Israel, and the Holy Spirit was upon him. And it had been revealed to him by the Holy Spirit that he would not see death before he had seen the Lord's Christ. So he came by the Spirit into the temple. And when the parents brought in the Child Jesus, to do for Him according to the custom of the law, 28 he took Him up in his arms and blessed God.*

And Simeon said, "Lord, now you are letting your servant depart in peace, according to Your word, for my eyes have seen Your salvation which You have prepared before the face of all peoples! A light to bring revelation to the Gentiles, And the glory of Your people Israel!" Then Simeon blessed them and said to Mary His mother, "Behold, this Child is destined for the fall and rising of many in Israel, and for a sign which will be spoken against (yes, a sword will pierce through your own soul also), that the thoughts of many hearts may be revealed."

"I suppose you want to be Simeon too, my darling Little Star?" said the Lord.

"No, sir!" said Little Star. "He's old and about to die! No, I'm cool right now."

Consolation: /ˌkänsəˈlāSH(ə)n/
comfort received by a person after a loss or disappointment. sympathy, compassion, pity

And the word of the Lord in Luke 2:36–38 reads:

> *Now there was one, Anna, a prophetess, the daughter of Phanuel, of the tribe of Asher. She was of a great age, and had lived with a husband seven years from her virginity, and this woman was a widow of about eighty-four years, who did not depart from the temple, but served God with fastings and prayers night and day. And coming in that instant she gave thanks to the Lord, and spoke of Him to all those who looked for redemption in Jerusalem.*

"I am old too," said Anna the **prophetess**. "I have been widowed for eighty-four years. But that has not stopped me from fasting, praying, and serving my God. I love giving Him thanksgiving and praise! Hallelujah to my Savior Jesus Christ, born the King of kings and the Lord of lords!"

Well?" said the Lord to Little Star.

"Pass," said Little Star.

"Merry Christmas my cute, adorable, and precious Little Star!" said the Lord.

Little Star, still feeling very sad, said, "I'm sorry Lord, but I don't feel so merry. It's because I don't feel as important as everyone else, including Simeon and Anna. All I ever wanted to do was shine. That's all, just shine. Oh yeah, and be significant, relevant, important, and a big deal. I neglected to tell you I also wanted to be very **irresistible** too, but I thought I might be asking for too much. Lord, I feel like I'm getting smaller. I'm disappearing because no one sees me! I'm heading with a one-way ticket to the land of "Not Important Enough!" Oh Lord, it's so upsetting to be me!"

Prophetess: ˈ/präfətəs/
1. a woman who speaks for God, by divine inspiration. 2. a woman who foretells future events

"My beautiful and My precious, My lovely and My adorable Little Star, don't you know, you have ALWAYS shined in My eyes just the way you are! Don't you see, My precious, you don't have to be something or somebody you're not because I created you to be different. And different is very special, which makes you so significant, so relevant, very uncommon, and so beautifully unique in all your being. You are important to Me because you matter to Me. Through the gift of my Son, everyone and everything I created shines in their OWN special way. Little Star, you are one of my most precious creations. You are My very own, 'Christmas Star!'"

Then the Heavenly Host shouted and proclaimed on one accord with a loud voice, "You are His creation, Little Star! You are a reflection of His handiwork! We see you, Little Star! We see you shining very bright! We see you Little Star!"

"I see you, Little Star!" said the moon! "We see you too!" said all the other stars! Their words echoed throughout the entire galaxy! "And even I see you, Little Star!" said planet Pluto, still showing off!

"Oops, we mean, Christmas Star!" **harken** the angel.

Little Star slowly looked all around and above her. She couldn't believe what her ears had just heard. She was so startled by the **proclamation** that she barely could speak. She whispered, "You see me? You all really…see me? You see me shining like a, like a…Christmas Star?"

"Like a significant, relevant, important yet very uncommon, unique, and beautiful Christmas Star', who is a very BIG deal and irresistible too! Yes, we see you, Christmas Star!" declared the angels.

"Oh my," said Little Star frizzled and frazzled! "I don't think I can breathe right now! I feel like something is coming over me. I think I'm going to faint. I feel like something is happening to me! I feel like, I feel like…*I'm SHINING!!!*" Little Star instantly became Christmas Star! with beautiful Christmas colors of red, green, and gold shining beautifully and brightly. Little Star gladly accepted who she is, was, and always will be! Special! Relevant. And a very BIG DEAL! Created by the Most High God! She was so full of joy and merriment that she started rejoicing happily with singing and dancing!

Proclamation:
präklə'māSH(ə)n· A public or official announcement of an important matter.

"This little light of mine, I'm gonna let it shine, let it shine, let it shine, let it shine! Whew! Oh my gosh!" she said as she tried to catch her breath! She found the strength to continue on joyfully! "Everywhere I go, I'm gonna let it shine, let it shine, let it shine, let it shine!" She fanned herself wildly, sat down, then got right back up again quickly, and continued singing and dancing! "Hide it under a bushel? NO! I'm gonna let it shine, let it shine, let it shine, LET IT SHIIIIIIIIIINE!!!"

And she KNEW exactly just where she wanted to shine the most! Christmas Star went right over the baby Jesus, beaming and, of course, shining!

"Oh, what a Holy Night!" said the Lord. And the angels sang, danced, and rejoiced! The entire heavenly host, as in heaven and now on earth, celebrated the birth of Jesus Christ on Christmas Day!

Merry Christmas

The End

In **memory** *of* **my** *parents,* **Charlie** *and* **Christine** *Norwood*

Highlighted Words to Add to Your Extensive Vocabulary!

Firmament: The firmament is the structure above the atmosphere, conceived as a vast solid dome.

Handiwork: Something that One has made or done.

Infinite: Limitless or endless in space, extent, or size; impossible to measure or calculate.

Omniscient: Mainly in religion, is the capacity to know everything that there is to know.

Significant: Sufficiently great or important to be worthy of attention; noteworthy.

Relevant: Appropriate to the current time, period, or circumstances; of contemporary interest.

Impoverish: The state or condition of having little or no money, goods, or means of support; being poor.

Decree: A formal and authoritative order, especially one having the force of law.

Census: An official count or survey of a population, typically recording various details of individuals.

Lodge: Stay or sleep in another person's house, paying money for one's accommodations.

Inn: An establishment providing accommodations, food, and drink, especially for travelers.

Pleasantry: A short polite conversation before the serious conversation.

Reluctantly: When you do something reluctantly, you don't really want to do it.

Woefully: Full of woe; wretched; unhappy and sad.

Omnipotent: Having all power over everything.

Impending: Close (at hand), near, nearing, approaching, about to happen.

Merciful: Coming as a mercy; bringing someone relief from something unpleasant.

Swaddling: Wrap (someone, especially a baby) in garments or cloth.

Anthem: A rousing or uplifting song identified with a particular group, body, or cause.

Laud: Praise (a person or their achievements) highly, especially in a public context.

Grammy: A Grammy Award is an honor awarded by the Recording Academy to recognize outstanding achievement in the music industry.

Contentment: A state of happiness and satisfaction.

Reconciled: To cause (a person) to accept or be resigned to something not desired.

Majesty: Greatness, royal power regal, lofty, or stately dignity; imposing character; grandeur.

Partake: Join in (an activity).

Proclaim: Announce officially or publicly.

Sentiments: A thought, opinion, or idea based on a feeling about a situation, or a way of thinking.

Marveled: Be filled with wonder or astonishment; awe.

Shear: Cut the wool off (a sheep or other animal).

Queasy: Nauseated; feeling sick.

Frankincense: An aromatic gum resin obtained from an African tree and burned as incense.

Myrrh: A fragrant gum resin obtained from certain trees and used in perfumery, medicines, and incense.

Irresistible: Too attractive and tempting to be resisted.

Harken: Attend, hark, hear, listen, heed, mind.

Merry Christmas

About the Author

Mrs. Chandra Felisa Wallace has been married to and in love with her boyfriend Demetrius John Wallace Sr. for twenty-nine years. Together they have four wonderful, beautiful children, Cymone, DJ, De'Von, and De'Andre Wallace. Chandra started her love of writing when she was in the second grade, writing poetry. She writes everything now from health and wellness blogs to advertisements and plays at her church. Out of Chandra's love of all things Christmas, she wrote and directed, The Christmas Star as a children's play. It was performed by the children's ministry of Grace Bible Fellowship of Antioch to rave reviews. Chandra thought it was one of the corniest plays she had written to date until she heard the voice of the Holy Spirit telling her to do something with it. Changes and revisions were made, and what evolved was a delightful, inspiring children's book! She has always loved reading and words, thus, compelling her to inspire children to develop their vocabulary with highlighted words defined in the back of the book. Her interesting take of the biblical account of the birth of Jesus is to help children know the real reason for the season and to convey a message of self-acceptance and self-worth within. God is love. And with the love of Jesus Christ in Chandra's heart, it has manifested itself in every page written in this lovely, awe-inspiring book.

9 781642 582819